Nanuk

LORD OF THE ICE

BRIAN J. HEINZ
paintings by GREGORY MANCHESS

Dial Books for Young Readers New York

For my wife, Judy, who loves the world in winter
—B.J.H.

For Tricia: wintersoul, snowangel
—G.M.

Published by Dial Books for Young Readers
A member of Penguin Putnam Inc.
375 Hudson Street / New York, New York 10014

Library of Congress Cataloging in Publication Data
Heinz, Brian J., date.
Nanuk: lord of the ice/ by Brian J. Heinz; paintings by Gregory Manchess.—1st ed.
p.   cm.
Summary: As a huge polar bear hunts seals and a walrus for food to keep
himself alive, he is in turn hunted by a young human.
ISBN 0-8037-2194-3 (trade)—ISBN 0-8037-2195-1 (lib. bdg.)
1. Polar bears—Juvenile fiction. [1. Polar bears—Fiction.
2. Bears—Fiction. 3. Arctic animals—Fiction. 4. Inuit—Fiction.]
I. Manchess, Gregory, ill. II. Title.
PZ10.3.H31765Nan 1998   [E]—DC21   97-26670   CIP   AC

The art for this book was prepared using oil paints on canvas,
and the title was hand-lettered by Mr. Manchess.

Author's Note

The polar bear is a living symbol of the arctic. It is solitary, mysterious, powerful, intensely curious, and highly intelligent.

For centuries this impressive animal has been tied to the culture and mythology of the arctic native peoples. To the Inuit and Inupiat the polar bear is known as *nanuk*, and it was a vital source of food, clothing, and implements. The bear is honored in the native stories, poetry, and songs, and is also known as the ice bear, the sea bear, and the ever-wandering-bear. Often boys were not considered true hunters until they had killed their first polar bear.

In times past, when the polar bear was hunted in traditional methods using dogs and hand weapons, its population was not threatened. However, in the 1960's trophy hunters swarmed into the remote arctic landscape with aircraft, snowmobiles, and high-powered rifles. The bear's numbers declined at an alarming rate, and in 1965 it was declared endangered by the International Union for the Conservation of Nature and Natural Resources.

In 1973 an international agreement was signed to protect the polar bear and the arctic environment. (Hunting is still allowed in traditional ways by the native people, but is limited and carefully regulated.) Today illegal hunting by poachers still threatens this majestic bear, but its greatest threats are the industrial pollutants that have found their way into the arctic food chains.

Presently the polar bear is safe, with a worldwide population estimated at between 30,000 and 40,000 bears. With people's renewed respect for the pristine arctic wilderness, Nanuk will roam the ice for ages to come.

An arctic wind whistled across the vast expanse of ice dusted with snow. Sculpted and polished by wind and wave, the massive, jagged chunks spilled over each other as Nanuk padded quietly toward open water, miles beyond. He was hungry.

Nanuk stopped, his white body just another piece of the icy jigsaw puzzle that was the arctic wilderness. Then, in silent grace, nine feet of bear rose upward and balanced motionless.

His eyes blinked against gusts of frigid air, and his head turned slowly from side to side as his black nose keened the wind. A trace of a faraway-something in the breeze met his nostrils. It was *natchik*. Seals.

Nanuk dropped to the ice with a short grunt, turned north, and walked with the determined pace of Nanuk the Hunter.

Thirty miles away, another hunter arose. The boy crawled from his igloo with eight leather harnesses over his arm. Mukluks warmed his feet. Dressed in bearskin leggings, parka, and sealskin mittens trimmed in fox fur, only his face showed he was *inuk*, human.

The hunting sled lay on its side, and as the boy approached, the snowy surface around him exploded to life with excited dogs. Using a pad of polar bear fur, he brushed the sled runners with water. While it froze and slickened the runners, he harnessed the dogs.

Elsewhere, Nanuk the Ever-Wandering-Bear paced over the ice. A trio of arctic foxes scampered up, like squires attending their knight, to escort Nanuk to the hunting ground. As he had often done before, Nanuk turned, lunged, and snarled a warning at the foxes. Only when they had backed off did he turn again and head on.

So Nanuk proceeded, with the foxes shadowing his every move. When Nanuk stopped, they stopped. When Nanuk sat, they sat. And when the bear had eaten, the foxes would eat.

Nanuk halted as a dark form poked above a crooked circle in the ice. The breathing hole of a ringed seal. Once. Twice. Three times the cautious seal surfaced, each time looking in a new direction, before hauling its body out onto the ice.

Nanuk kept his distance and waited. The seal raised its head and looked about. For a moment the seal stared directly at Nanuk but did not see him. Nanuk had become the Ice Bear.

When the seal dropped its head and closed its eyes, Nanuk stalked over the ice while the distant foxes trotted impatiently back and forth. Just fifty feet from the seal, Nanuk's next step sent a faint tremor through the ice. The seal plunged into the breathing hole and vanished.

It had happened before. Nanuk treaded in whispered steps to the opening, where he lay down to wait with his nose and massive paws inches from the edge, his eyes fixed upon the water's surface.

For an hour he lay silent and still but for the ruffling of his fur in the breeze and the slow rise and fall of his breathing. The foxes, too, sat quietly in the distance.

The water rippled as another seal surfaced. *Swack!* With one lightning swipe Nanuk snapped the seal's neck. He closed his jaws over the seal's shoulder, lifting it easily onto the ice. The foxes hopped up, yapping and parading in circles as if in celebration.

Miles away the Inuk hunter stood by his sled amidst the furious barking of dogs anxious to be off. But the hunter took a moment to secure his *satkut,* his weapons. He slipped his bow and arrows under the *amik,* a caribou skin tied to the sled's frame. He tugged on the line of his harpoon and examined his lance blade, nodding approval at its razor edge, then tucked these weapons away too.

The hunter shouted to the team, and the dogs leaped against their harnesses. The sled burst forward, skittering across the ice behind the dogs.

"Ayee!" Balanced on the runners at the rear of the sled, the Inuk urged the dogs onward with feverish shouts.

Meanwhile Nanuk clamped his dead seal down under his right forefoot and skinned the carcass, tearing out the blubber with raking claws, staining the ice crimson. It was the blubber that he swallowed in ragged chunks. It was the blubber that gave him strength, that protected him from temperatures of seventy degrees below zero. It was the blubber that kept him alive.

But it was a small seal for such a big bear. So Nanuk headed to the edge of the sea with hopes of a second seal to satisfy his hunger, while the foxes raced to the carcass and ate their fill of the tough, muscled flesh that Nanuk left behind.

By now the boy hunter had picked up the trail of the great bear. His dogs were wild with the scent. As they turned tightly in pursuit to run in the bear's tracks, the sled lurched and the runners cut deeply into the surface, sending up sprays of shaved ice.

The Inuk hopped from the sled. Running lightly alongside, he grasped the frame and tilted the sled onto one runner to guide it into the turn. Seconds later the hunter leaped back onto the sled as it gathered speed, weaving among cracks, ridges, and tall shards of ice, racing to the sea. Racing to Nanuk.

By noon Nanuk had reached the ocean. It was a cold, dark ocean of crooked waves and whitecaps under dull clouds. Nanuk rambled along the edge of the ice and came upon *aivik,* the walrus. He watched the walrus rock back and forth on massive flippers. Great folds of skin on its thick neck shuddered as the walrus slammed its chest onto the ice, threatening Nanuk. Then the walrus shook its fierce, yellowed tusks, reared its whiskered head back, and bellowed out a thousand pounds of anger.

Nanuk stood his ground. In defiance he lowered his head, curled up his lips, and roared back. Then he skirted past the walrus, for his sensitive nose had already found the favored smell of *ugruk,* the bearded seal.

Nanuk saw the fat seal diving for fish a scant hundred yards beyond the ice blanket. From times past, Nanuk knew the seal's diving patterns, and at the seal's next plunge Nanuk made his move. Dropping to his elbows, he crept over the ice, stopping each time the seal broke the surface to breathe.

So it went until Nanuk reached the water and flattened himself over the ice like a shadow. He knew that any noise or sudden movement would announce him to the seal, sending it racing away. And he knew he could not outswim the seal. The bear would rely on stealth, on cunning, and on the whims of the currents.

At the seal's next dive Nanuk slid, smoothly, silently, over the lip of ice and into the water. The hollow hairs of his thick fur and a dense layer of fat blocked out the frigid sea while he floated motionless, as if dead.

The seal reappeared and glanced briefly at the bear. But with legs splayed outward and his chin on the surface, Nanuk was nothing more than another piece of lifeless, drifting ice in a frozen world. Nanuk had become the Sea Bear.

It took patience, this drifting, this waiting for a breath of wind, a surge of current, or the slap of a wave. But the elements were with him, and soon Nanuk was only eight feet from the seal's feeding spot. The seal rolled over several times, dashed in small circles, then dove again.

Suddenly it was there before him. With savage speed the bear's crushing jaws closed on the seal's head and shook it from side to side.

In moments Nanuk had paddled back to the ice. He stood over the seal's body as the water fell from his fur. But an enemy was approaching quickly, and Nanuk turned to face the noise on the wind.

The Inuk and his dogs could see the great bear now. The hunter stepped hard on the snow brake and brought the sled to a brief stop. He cut three dogs loose and they raced to Nanuk with outstretched bodies. In no time they were upon him.

Nanuk braced himself and snarled as the dogs closed around him on three sides, taking turns to dash in and nip at his heels and hindquarters, sometimes tearing out a mouthful of fur. No matter how quickly Nanuk turned to repel one dog, another was behind him. And now the Inuk had arrived. The sled came to an abrupt stop, and the hunter freed the remaining dogs that closed the circle on Nanuk.

Nanuk fought back the dogs blocking his path to the sea as the Inuk lifted the caribou hide that covered his weapons, and removed his lance.

Nanuk had only seconds, and the sea was his only escape. As the Inuk approached and raised his lance, Nanuk made a desperate charge toward the water. The surprised dogs skipped aside as Nanuk leaped over them and crashed into the sea.

With Nanuk in the water, the lance was now useless. The hunter tossed it down and snatched his harpoon.

Nanuk paddled steadily away as the hunter raised the harpoon, and drove it stiffly through the air. The point cut across the great bear's shoulder, sending a thin curl of blood into the water. The bear roared and turned his head to bite at the pain. But the barb did not root itself. The wound would heal, and Nanuk was soon out of range of the hunter's weapon.

The Inuk hauled in his empty line. He would settle for Nanuk's dead seal. Amidst the furious yelping of his dogs, the hunter raised his hands high into the air and shouted praises to the great bear's courage.

Nanuk swam ten miles across open water. A roaring gale blew over the sea, whipping the water to froth. Before him floated a place of rest, an enormous chunk of glacial ice. Anxious to reach it, his strokes became quicker and more powerful.

Finally, Nanuk's paws hit the ice. His claws dug in and he dragged his tired body out of the water.

Whipped by the whirling snow, Nanuk climbed atop the icy mass and threw back his head. His roar was lifted and carried on the arctic wind.

Nanuk was wild. Nanuk was free.

And Nanuk was still Lord of the Ice.